# A FOX
# GOT MY SOCKS

# For Charlie Everton Bingham

*A Red Fox Book*

*Published by Random House Children's Books*
*20 Vauxhall Bridge Road, London SW1V 2SA*

*A division of Random House UK Ltd*
*London Melbourne Sydney Auckland*
*Johannesburg and agencies throughout the world*

*First published in 1992 by Hutchinson Children's Books*

*Red Fox edition 1994*

*© Hilda Offen 1992*

*Designed by Paul Welti*

*Printed in China*

*RANDOM HOUSE UK Limited Reg. No. 954009*

*ISBN 0 09 999780 0*

# A FOX
# GOT MY SOCKS
## Hilda Offen

*RED FOX*

Yesterday
was washing day.

*Pretend to wash*

My clothes flip-flapped
and blew away.

*Flap arms*

A cat got my hat.

*Touch head with both hands*

A fox got my socks.

*Touch both feet*

A goat got my coat.

*Pretend to do up buttons*

An owl got my towel.

*Pretend to flap towel*

'Oh no!' said the pig.
'These pants are too big!'

*Pretend to hold up pants*

And the bear gave a snort:
'This jumper's too short!'

*Pull jumper up*

Two baby llamas
were in my pyjamas

*Touch chest and knee*

And where was my scarf?
Wrapped round a giraffe!

*Pretend to wrap scarf*

But the sun was so hot,

*Fan face*

I said, 'Keep what you've got.

*Hold out arms*

I'm perfectly happy …

... to stay in my nappy!'

*Dance around*

# Some bestselling Red Fox picture books

THE BIG ALFIE AND ANNIE ROSE STORYBOOK
*by Shirley Hughes*
OLD BEAR
*by Jane Hissey*
OI! GET OFF OUR TRAIN
*by John Burningham*
DON'T DO THAT!
*by Tony Ross*
NOT NOW, BERNARD
*by David McKee*
ALL JOIN IN
*by Quentin Blake*
THE MOON'S REVENGE
*by Joan Aiken and Alan Lee*
BAD BORIS GOES TO SCHOOL
*by Susie Jenkin-Pearce*
WE CAN SAY NO!
*by David Pithers and Sarah Greene*
MATILDA
*by Hilaire Belloc and Posy Simmonds*
WILLY AND HUGH
*by Anthony Browne*
THE WINTER HEDGEHOG
*by Ann and Reg Cartwright*
A DARK, DARK TALE
*by Ruth Brown*
HARRY, THE DIRTY DOG
*by Gene Zion and Margaret Bloy Graham*
DR XARGLE'S BOOK OF EARTHLETS
*by Jeanne Willis and Tony Ross*
JAKE
*by Deborah King*